Tag!

Crabtree Publishing Company
www.crabtreebooks.com
1-800-387-7650

PMB 16A, 350 Fifth Ave.
Suite 3308,
New York, NY

616 Welland Ave.
St. Catharines, ON
L2M 5V6

Published by Crabtree Publishing in 2010

Series Editor: Jackie Hamley
Editors: Melanie Palmer, Reagan Miller
Series Advisor: Dr. Hilary Minns
Series Designer: Peter Scoulding
Editorial Director: Kathy Middleton

Text © Ann Bryant 2008
Illustration © Kirsteen H. Jones 2008

The rights of the author and the illustrator
of this Work have been asserted.

For Juliette with love
and all best wishes - A.B.

First published in 2008
by Franklin Watts
(A division of Hachette
Children's Books)

Printed in Canada/032020/
EN20200214

**Library and Archives Canada
Cataloguing in Publication**

Bryant, Ann
	Tag! / Ann Bryant ; illustrated by Kirsteen H.
Jones.

(Tadpoles)
ISBN 978-0-7787-3869-5 (bound).--
ISBN 978-0-7787-3900-5 (pbk.)

	1. Readers (Primary). 2. Readers--Tag games.
I. Jones, Kirsteen H. II. Title. III. Series: Tadpoles
(St. Catharines, Ont.)

PE1117.T33 2009f   428.6   C2009-903987-7

**Library of Congress
Cataloging-in-Publication Data**

Bryant, Ann.
	Tag! / by Ann Bryant ; illustrated by Kirsteen H.
Jones.
	p. cm. -- (Tadpoles)
	Summary: Pig brothers Sid, Mick, and Dan try to
escape from a determined Wolf.
	ISBN 978-0-7787-3900-5 (pbk.) -- ISBN
978-0-7787-3869-5 (reinforced library binding)
	[1. Pigs--Fiction. 2. Wolves--Fiction.] I. Jones,
Kirsteen H., ill. II. Title. III. Series.

PZ7.B8298Tag 2010
[E]--dc22

2009025296

Tag!

by Ann Bryant

Illustrated by Kirsteen H. Jones

Crabtree Publishing Company

www.crabtreebooks.com

Ann Bryant

"I've only got a cat for a pet, but I think a pig might be quite nice, especially one like Sid the Pig who would do the cooking for me!"

Kirsteen H. Jones

"Creating the characters for this re-telling of the three little pigs story was lots of fun, especially the wolf with his hungry expression!"

Sid the pig was cooking when ...

...Wolf came to
the door.

Sid ran to Dan's house.

Wolf chased him.

"Quick! Run!" said Sid.
"Wolf is coming!"

"Ha, ha!" laughed Wolf.

Sid and Dan
ran and ran ...

... to Mick's house.

But Mick forgot to lock the door.

The three pigs raced up the chimney.

19

But they did not get far

"Tag!" said Wolf.
"Now you're IT!"

Notes for adults

TADPOLES are structured to provide support for early readers. The stories may also be used by adults for sharing with young children.

Starting to read alone can be daunting. **TADPOLES** help by providing visual support and repeating high frequency words and phrases. These books will both develop confidence and encourage reading and rereading for pleasure.

If you are reading this book with a child, here are a few suggestions:

1. Make reading fun! Choose a time to read when you and the child are relaxed and have time to share the story.
2. Talk about the story before you start reading. Look at the cover and the blurb. What might the story be about? Why might the child like it?
3. Encourage the child to reread the story, and to retell the story in their own words, using the illustrations to remind them what has happened.
4. Discuss the story and see if the child can relate it to their own experiences, or perhaps compare it to another story they know.
5. Give praise! Children learn best in a positive environment.